Rocks In My Socks And Rainbows Too

Written by Lavelle Carlson

Illustrated by Lucas Adams

A Phonemic Awareness Tale

Rocks in My Socks
and Rainbows Too
Phonemic Awareness Tale #3
Copyright 2003

Written by Lavelle Carlson
Illustrated by Lucas Adams

Inquiries should be addressed to:
Children's Publishing
201 Woodland Park
Georgetown, Texas 78628

First Edition

ISBN: 0-9725803-2-8
Library of Congress Catalog Card Number: 2003097630

Carlson, Lavelle
    Rocks in my socks and rainbows too / written by Lavelle Carlson ;
illustrated by Lucas Adams. - 1st ed. - Georgetown, Tex. : Children's
Publishing, c2003.
    27 p. : col. ill. ; 29 cm.
    "A phonemic awareness tale"
    Summary: Young Corey is always bored until his friend Fox suggests he
play with his socks - which he finds a way to do on the way home! Entertains
while teaching phonemic awareness, skills and sounds targeted, and word and
syllable levels, and includes teacher information on phonemic awareness levels,
skills and sounds targeted, and word and syllable levels.
    ISBN: 0-9725803-2-8
    1. Boredom - Juvenile fiction. 2. Color - Juvenile fiction. 3. English
language - Diction - Juvenile fiction. 4. Auditory perception. 5. Speech
perception. 6. Reading (Primary). [[1. Boredom. 2. Color. 3. Stories in
rhyme.] I. Adams, Lucas Grillis, ill. II. Title.
[E]-dc2   2003097630

Although information herein is based on the author's extensive
experience and knowledge, it is not intended to substitute for
the services of qualified professionals.

Printed in Hong Kong

There once was a boy named Corey
who said, "Life is so-o-o boring."
His good friend Mr. Fox said,
"Play with your blocks."
"I don't have any blocks."
"Then play with your socks."
(What did Corey really do with his socks?)

Dedicated to all the children who love to fill
their pockets with rocks.

Red rocks, yellow rocks, green rocks, white rocks, purple rocks, pink rocks, black rocks, orange rocks, gray rocks, gold rocks. Ooh, I like the red rocks.

Moo, moo. I don't see blue, do you?

5

13

16

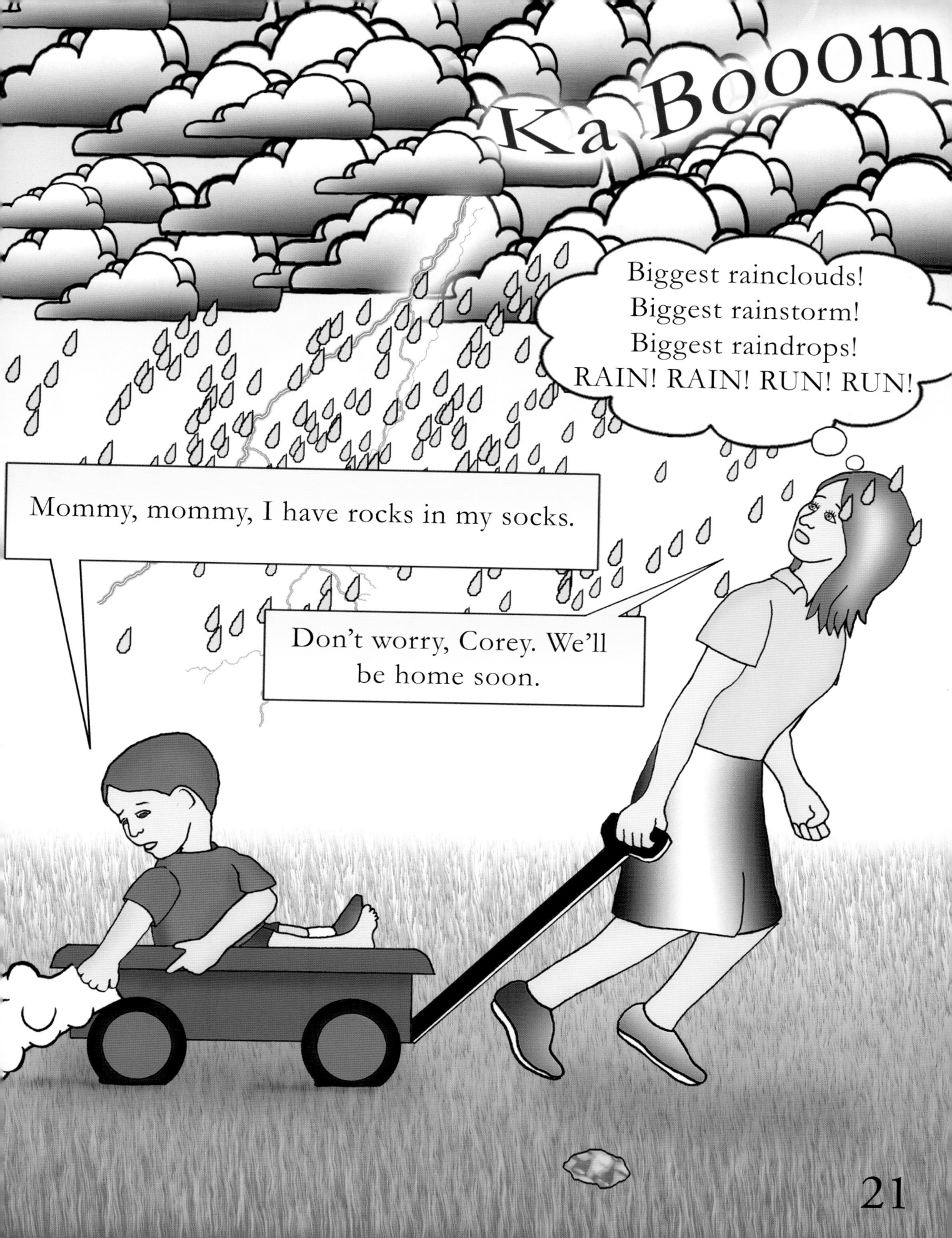

23

THE END...

Big   Bigger   Biggest

Small   Smaller   Smallest

Big   Bigger   Biggest

Small   Smaller   Smallest

PHONEMIC AWARENESS:

Definition: The ability to create new words by adding, deleting, shifting, and substituting speech sounds.

Levels:
1. Sound localization: Identifying the source of the sound.
2. Sound discrimination: Ability to tell the difference between two similar speech sounds in isolation; i.e., /b/ or /d/ or in words; i.e., "bean" or "dean".
3. Word awareness: Identifying the number of words in a sentence. There are six words in the sentence, "The dog is big and brown."
4. Syllable awareness: Identifying the number of syllables in a word. The word "mother" has two syllables. The word "popsicle" has three syllables.
5. Manipulation (add, delete, shift, and substitute) of sounds to create new words. "Mat," take away /m/ (sound) = "at."
"Mat," add /s/ (sound) = "mats."
"Mats" with the /t/ and /s/ (sounds) shifted = "mast."
"Mat" with /k/ (sound, letter "c") substituted for /m/ (sound) = "cat."

The same changes can be applied to syllables: i.e., "depart" plus "ment" = "department."

PHONEMIC AWARENESS SKILLS TARGETED:

Word level, syllable level, sound level

SOUNDS TARGETED:

/bl/, /b/, /p/, /kl/ (spelling "cl"), /r/, /gr/, /m/, /s/, /g/

BASIC LANGUAGE SKILLS TARGETED:

Attribute: Colors

Comprehension: Who, What, When, Where, Why?

Early inference skills using pictures: "The clouds are getting bigger. What will happen?" "Why is the sun almost gone?" "Why is the sock getting big and bigger?" "Why are the wagon tires getting flat?" "Did the mother know that Corey was putting socks in his rocks?" "Who is asking questions in the story?" (The animals are.) "What was Cory riding in?"

Read the story each day to be able to go through the entire sequence of exercises. In the beginning use pictures or other manipulatives and point to each as you say them. After the students respond, count the pictures and congratulate the students for helping you. After doing this exercise a few times during the semester with different stories, discontinue using the pictures and manipulatives and try to get the students to come up with other methods of counting or remembering the words you say; i.e., use your fingers, clap your hands, etc.

***Phonemic awareness activities are complemented by whole language activities. Talk about the story with the students and ask comprehension questions; i.e., who, what is that, what is she or he doing, when, where, why. While reading ask them what is happening in the pictures. As the pictures change on succeeding pages, ask them what they think will happen.

Although phonemic awareness develops in sequence beginning from word to syllable to speech sound awareness, it is possible to combine the levels during a session to accommodate varying skill levels.

Word Level:

Teacher: When you hear the name of a color pretend to color a picture. Pause slightly after each word to give the students time to respond.

    Example: red, circle, blue, chair, boy, yellow, etc.

Teacher: "How many words did I name?" (Allow one student ay a time to drop rocks or something resembling rocks in a container, preferably one that gives noise feedback. Have the students count their rocks after each group of words.)

Red rocks. (2)
Play with rocks. (3)
I like red rocks. (4)

Teacher: "Tell me if these words are same or different."
Red - red (same)
Gold - pink (different)

Play "Hide the word." You can use the pictures in the beginning to help the students get the idea. Again, at some point discontinue using the pictures. Also, clap your hands for each word when it is said and also when it is omitted.)

Teacher: Say "rock - rain."
Students: "Rock - rain."
Teacher: Now tell me what I forgot to say. "(clap and omit rock) - rain."
Students: "Rock."

Teacher: After you have read the story to the students tell them you will read page 2 and they are to help you when you cannot read the next word.

> Example: "Blue (pause), red (pause), yellow (pause), green (pause), white (pause), purple (pause), pink (pause), black (pause), orange (pause), gray (pause), gold (pause)." The students should respond "rocks" each time you pause.

Teacher: Help me finish these sentences: (This can be done during the reading of the story after the children become familiar with the story.)

> Mommy, Mommy, I have rocks in my (socks).
> If you don't have blocks, play with (rocks).
> Gold rocks. Ooh, I like the (gold rocks).

Teacher: I am going to say a silly sentence and you help me by making it sound right.

> I put a rock in my clock. (I put a rock in my sock.)
> I have a fox in my sock. (I have a rock in my sock.)

Syllable level: Activities can be similar to above exercises but with parts of words instead of whole words.

Teacher: How many times does you chin move when you say these words? (Demonstrate by opening your mouth with exaggeration. A mirror helps.)

> Purple (2)
> Red (1)
> Yellow (2)

Teacher: "What color am I saying? When I clap it means I forgot part of the word."

> "pur" (teacher claps) - children's response: "purple"
> (teacher claps) "range" - children's response: "orange"
> "Yel" (teacher claps) - children's response: "yellow"

Speech sound awareness:

Teacher: "I am going to talk like a robot and you try to tell me what I said." (As you say the word, pause between each sound. If the students do not guess correctly, make the pauses shorter. Let the students take turns being the robot. They will first draw a card that has a color on one side and will say that color as you demonstrated with the pauses.)

> "R – e – d What color did I say?" (Children's response: "red")
> "G – r - ay What color did I say?" (Children's response: "gray")